CAPTURED
BY HIS
Glory

P. FELIX EFIRI

Captured By His Glory

ISBN: 9798407064343

First Printing 2010
Copyright © GLIN Publications

Email: limng@rocketmail.com
               felix4us2003@yahoo.com
               felix4us2003@gmail.com

SMS/Whatsapp: +234-(0)806-042-1226
                    +234-(0)902-019-8571

All scripture quotations are taken from the King James Version of the Bible, except otherwise stated.

TABLE OF CONTENTS

You need revelation as key to experience His glory, as an ambassador of the kingdom. Your dignity is determined by your depth of insight. We have a very enviable inheritance in Christ as partakers of His divine nature, having escaped the corruption that is in the world. Your inheritance in Christ can only be delivered to you through the revelation of the Word of God [Acts 20:32].

> "Gird thy sword upon thy thigh, O most mighty, with thy glory and thy majesty. And in thy majesty ride prosperously because of truth and meekness and righteousness; and thy right hand shall teach thee terrible things."
>
> **[Psalms 45:3-4]**

CAPTURED BY HIS GLORY conveys deep truths with simplicity. It is a spiritual plumb to detect where we are not straight as we profess Christianity.

REV. C. KALU UKPAI
CGMi, Enerhen District Headquarters, Warri

*   *   *   *   *

I must say this is a very good book written from deep

inspiration, and a burdened heart towards the latter day revival.

It is a must read for all believers and all who sought to have an encounter and experience; most especially for ministers who are still operating on past glory.

Thanks my Brother, P. Felix for this gift to Christendom!

REV. GODFREY OKODUGHA
Director, Expression of the HeartMagazine

INTRODUCTION

" Some are still preaching, singing and prophesying, and God has turned off their microphones! That is why we are hearing a 'leftover' word because they have no fresh bread! They do not even realize God has raised a David, a NO NAME to take their place! They refused to obey, so, those God had hidden are about to come to the forefront." – Jennifer Sanders.

CAPTURED BY HIS GLORY is a book written for the individual Christian, willing to take advantage of the times we are in. It is written to expose those God had hidden and prepared for forefront. It carries within itself the ingredient to spark, and set you ablaze for God. Until you are captured by His Glory, Christianity would be a mere religion to you. Religion is a burden difficult to bear; it stinks and makes its practitioners exist without living. Religion presents you titles, and denies you mantle for kingdom assignment.

Here is a treasure trove in your hand. Read and be inspired by the lines. Do not be selfish with the truth you are about to experience, kindly share it!

1

KNOW IT

In its definition, the Oxford Advance Learner's Dictionary presents Glory as "fame, praise or honour, and great beauty."

Glory is one of the most commonly used words in the Bible. In the Old Testament, it is used to translate several Hebrew words, including "Hod" and "Kabod," and in the New Testament, it is used to translate the Greek word "doxa."

Kabod

The Hebrew word "Kabod" originally means weight or heaviness; the same word is then used to express importance, honour and majesty. Greek version of the Bible translated this concept with the word "doxa," which was then used extensively in the New Testament as well. Doxa originally means judgment, opinion, and by extension, good reputation, honour, etc.

Glory

Glory (Shekinah or Kabod) is also viewed as the expression of divine attributes collectively. It is the unfolded fullness of divine perfections, "the very image" of His substance (ibid) [Vincent word studies of the New Testament].

          CAPTURED BY HIS GLORY

Capture

Expugno is a Latin word that means, "To capture, overcome, subdue and gain." The Greek word [Zogreo] puts it thus: "to take hold or held captive, to entrap." In extension, captureisto attract, take control, catch, imprisoned, etc.

Captured by His Glory

This is to be attracted, gained, overcome, subdued, imprisoned, or controlled by God's presence, weight/heaviness [Matthew 11 : 29-30], judgment, importance, fame, praise, great beauty, good reputation, honour and majesty.

Religious days

During the "religious days," the glory of God was resident in the Ark of the Covenant, laid in the most Holy place of the Tabernacle. This protocol was reversed by the finished work on Calvary [Matthew 27:51], giving everyone the privilege to be carriers [I Corinthians 6:19-20] of God's glory for His glory.

The difference

We are the same as a result of the finished work on Calvary; however, the difference is in the measure of glory and grace I am endowed with that you are not. The difference is in our office of assignment; it is what I know that you don't know; it is what I know and act that you know and didn't act on, which is a function of commitment, dedication and devotion. You can be "Kingdom favorite" and do greater works [John 14:12] than your role models and mentors, if you allow your life to be captured by His glory. Are you ready for greater works in enforcing the kingdom of God in your world? Let's go!

2

CAPTURED BY HIS GLORY

The glory of God is the visible manifestation of His presence, weight/heaviness, judgment, importance, fame, praise, good reputation, honour and majesty, through creation. You can be captured by God, and as well be captured by His glory.

To be captured by God

When Moses demanded to see the face of God as recorded in Exodus chapter thirty-three, God told him: "…you cannot see my face: for there shall no man see me, and live…"

Moses' demand to see the face of God revealed His quest to have an intimate knowledge of God's personality. To see the face of God is to have a clear sight of His nature, which is impossible in our mortal bodies. There is something about God's face that is too awesome for man to behold in the flesh.

To see the face of God is to be captured by God. To be captured by God is to be done with one's purpose on earth. It is to put off mortality for immortality. Moses did not see God as He is; that would have been the end of his work on earth. However, he was allowed to see the passing Glory of God; the after effect of His going by [Exodus 33:21-23].

It was recorded in Exodus 34:30-35 that: "…when Aaron and all the children of Israel saw Moses, behold, the skin of his face shone; and they were afraid to come nigh him…afterward all the children of Israel came nigh…and until Moses had done speaking with them, he put a veil on his face…" What a glory!

Captured by His Glory

Moses was one man captured by the glory of God. As powerful as the glory he was captured by, God still said:

> "And I will shake all the nations, and the desire of all nations shall come: and I will fill this house with glory, saith the LORD of hosts…the glory of this latter house shall be greater than of the former, saith the LORD of hosts…"
>
> **[Haggai 2:7,9]**

At many occasions in the Bible, God revealed His glory to certain extent to His people, most especially those He chose for His tasks. A vast majority of this super-ordinary people left their footprint on the shores of life. We have not stopped seeing and reading their legacies. You cannot be captured by the glory of God, and do not have your print in the Chronicle of men who enforced and are enforcing God's Kingdom on earth. Men like:

Smith Wigglesworth – the Apostle of faith and pioneer

of Pentecostal revival.

Dwight L. Moody— who lost his alcoholic father at age four, struggled in his early life, but known as the greatest evangelist in the nineteenth century.

Oral Roberts — A man who began life in poverty and nearly died of tuberculosis, but later became a televangelist and faith healer around the world; conducted more than three hundred healing crusades in six continents of the world.

T.L. Osborn — A Pentecostal evangelist and author of several books.

Billy Graham— An evangelist said to have preached in person to more people around the world than any other preacher in history. In 1993, more than 2.5 million souls stepped forward at his crusade to accept Jesus Christ as their Lord and personal savior; a spiritual adviser to twelve American presidents.

Kenneth E. Hagen— A man who suffered deformed heart and what was believed to be an incurable blood disease; not expected to live, and became bedfast at age sixteen, but became a preacher and pioneer of the Word of Faith Movement with Mark 11:23 as his favorite scripture; a

        CAPTURED BY HIS GLORY

part of the Voice of Healing Revival in the forties and fifties, along Oral Roberts, Gordon Lindsey and T.L. Osborn.

Martin Luther King, Jr.— A Pastor, activist and prominent leader in the African-American Civil Rights Movement; the youngest to receive the Nobel Peace Prize [at the time] for his work to end racial segregation and discrimination.

Arch Bishop Benson Idahosa— Rejected by his father and dumped in a rubbish bin by his mother, due to his unhealthy and fainting nature, but rose to be the man with FIRE IN HIS BONES, and great evangelist of faith, dynamic preacher with great works in Nigeria, Africa and the world at large.

And many others, too numerous to mention. What impact are you making that you would be remembered for?

What it cost

To be captured by His Glory is to lose your face for His Face; your beauty for His Beauty; your intellect for His Intellect; your wisdom for His Wisdom; your freedom for His Freedom; your will for His Will; your time for His Time; what you know for what He Knows. This was the exact act of the early Christians; they gave everything for the advancement of the Kingdom of God without exploiting one another; they were not respecters of persons, everybody was regarded as one [Acts 2:42-47].

It is unfortunate to note that the reverse of what the apostles demonstrated in their time is what we see in Christendom [today] as most ministers continue to strive for lordship rather than leadership, busy creating the "I am for Paul or Apollos" atmosphere, leaving members in chronic malnutrition; the result of this malnutrition is a 'neither hot nor cold Church;' a Church castrated, inflicted with fear and made to see what satan can do rather than what God can and has done; a Church that seek 'other things' first before God; a Church that follows after miracles, signs and wonders that is supposed to be her nature; a Church with dead conscious; a purposeless Church.

One day, a minister was preaching and said that the power of God is not manifesting in the Church because of the sins of the people; a people he had led for many years. While sin has its role, sin can't stop the manifest presence of God on earth; God is too committed to fulfilling His reclamation agenda by the Holy Spirit. I attribute the statement of that minister as a route to justify failure of leadership, misunderstanding of kingdom purpose, unwillingness to lose his face for God's Face, and inability to realize that God has

     CAPTURED BY HIS GLORY

turned off his microphone!

One of the reasons God manifested Himself in Jesus Christ was to redeem man from sin. Sin actually attracted Jesus to the world; it never stopped Him from performing and manifesting divine grace; sin never stopped the apostles from performing; sin never stopped the late Arch Bishop Benson Idahosa [of blessed memory] from performing; sin never stopped Pastor Chris Oyakhilome from manifesting divine abilities, rather, it motivated them to act. Wherever sin abounds is a priceless opportunity to preach the kingdom of God with power, without condemnation.

The way to make kingdom impact is in being captured by His glory. To be captured by His glory is to be His person, and you can't be His person without going through His process. It takes the whole of you to be captured by His Glory. To be captured by His Glory is to represent Him [Jehovah] on earth.

3

YOU:
AN AMBASSADOR

To be captured by His Glory is to represent Him on earth. You are not here to represent religion; religion is man invented and fuels division. You are here to represent the Kingdom of God. Every nation has ambassadors. An ambassador is the highest ranking diplomat that represents a nation, and usually accredited to a foreign government, or an international organization of which the "host," typically allows the ambassador control of a territory called embassy; staff, and even vehicles are accorded diplomatic immunity in the host country. The ambassadors' topmost interest is the nation he or she represents. He or she seeks first the interest of his or her nation before other things. The welfare of the ambassador is taken care of by the nation he or she represents.

As born again, blood washed, tongue speaking believer, you are God's ambassador, while the earth is your embassy, the local assembly where you worship is your consulate. Like earthly ambassadors; the glory of God captures you and make you a true representative of His kingdom on earth. Representing God means making Him first in your life and endeavors; making His interest your number one priority; attending to God first before any other thing; it is minding what God minds, irrespective of secular perspectives; it is proper alignment to God's agenda as enshrined in His word [the Bible] – Matthew 6:33,

> "But seek ye first the kingdom of God, and His righteousness; and all these things shall be added unto you."

This delivers the proper discernment and adequate empowerment you need for every good work.

Representing God is doing His Will rather than your will. It is bearing His burden rather than your burden [Matthew 11:29- 30]; working His orders rather than your orders, and speaking His interest rather than your interest. God takes full responsibility for the welfare of His ambassadors.

Who are you representing? God, mammon or self? It amazes me how some supposed ambassadors of the kingdom plan programs with the sole aim of what amount of money would be made after such programs. What would be of benefit to the people is almost often not considered. Giving is powerful, but condescending to the level of cajoling people so you can take from them, reveals your pettiness and proves that some things are not right with you. Who told you it is only when money is given one is blessed?

I attended a conference about two years ago, precisely 2008; to my greatest surprise, no fund was raised. The guest speaker [Pastor KK, as they called him], asked us to present before the altar whatever we are using for work; I remembered presenting a Bible, Biro and a few naira bills he prayed on and requested we take back. The word from that conference is still very much alive in me; it was what drove me to acquire my first landed property, measuring 1416.183 square metres.

The more people are cajoled, the poorer they become; this is my finding. Perhaps, they are not taught to give and how to attract more resources into their lives. God does not give wealth, but gives power to get wealth [Deuteronomy 8:18]. If they are taught and become captured by His glory, giving to their Pastors, kingdom projects as well as the needy would become a culture; they are better blessed in this situation. I have not said it is bad to sow seeds, it is absolutely good and a weapon in itself, but let the people be taught so they can engage with understanding. I understand the gospel of Jesus Christ is free, I also know it is not cheap. There is reward for every giving. A non-giving Christian is a disaster to his or herself.

You cannot be captured by His glory and engage in

   CAPTURED BY HIS GLORY

financial gimmicks; it simply reveals what representative you are; representing God, man or your pocket? Funds come so long as you remain a devout kingdom ambassador. God is committed to your welfare. Supernatural supply is real. "When God gives a vision, He makes the provision,"[Arch Bishop B.A. Idahosa]. Your craftiness is not required, His wisdom does it.

He needs your body

God is a Spirit being [John 4:24a]; He does not have a physical body; He needs your body; this is because, His topmost mission is to catch men alive and make them fishers of men [Matthew 4:19. Mark 16:15]. This has nothing to do with a craft or profession [even though they have their advantages], but anchored on availability! Usability in God's agenda rests on availability; you are usable to the level you are available.

Inasmuch as God need man; you need to understand He is the creator of "all," and can do without man, but he would not because by default, He made man especially for Himself. You don't just exist; neither are you a product of biological accident. You are a creation of purpose. You serve a unique purpose in God's interest.

Representing God is more than being a member of a Christian denomination. It is more than titles in church. It is more than being a Pastor or General Overseer [who do not even see]. It is more than performing the activities of God. Interestingly, you can perform the activities of God and not find Him. You can perform God's activities and not know Him. This is the true state of many a "church people." God can use you accomplish His interest, in certain circumstance, for His name sake and not regard you as one of His. Have you not read in Matthew 7:22-23?

> "Many will say to me in that day, Lord, Lord, have we not prophesied in thy name? And in thy name have cast out devils? And in thy name done many wonderful works? And then will I Profess unto them, I never knew you..."

Representing God is exhibiting His true nature [because He dwells in you]. You become a true reflection of His character [Galatians 5:22-23]. You see like Him; think like Him; wise like Him; talk like Him; love like Him; patient like Him, peaceful like Him, joyful like Him, accomplish tasks like Him and judge like Him [Isaiah 11:3]. All of these would not be until you "stop answering to Eli [I Samuel 3:4-10]" and start answering to God. This does not negate the role of Eli, because, at some point, you may need Eli to help identify the voice that calls.

     CAPTURED BY HIS GLORY

Answering to God is making yourself available. It is saying, "Here am I, LORD; do with me what you would. Use me for your glory. I am ready to work as your ambassador." This is a start of attracting Kingdom empowerment to reach nations awaiting your manifestation, "For the earnest expectation of the creation waiteth for manifestation of the sons of God, [Romans 8:19). Hallelujah!

4

HOW TO BE
CAPTURED
BY HIS GLORY

The principle of cause and effect states that for every effect, there is a cause. Nothing unfolds with the absence of nothing. A body is said to be at rest until an equivalent force acts on it. You would not have happened if something had not happened many years back. Every action produces equivalent consequence.

God can force His will on everyone, but He would not. He can, because He made everyone. He would not, because He respects everyone's right to choice [Deuteronomy 30:19. Joshua 24:15].

> "Then the elders of Israel gathered themselves together, and came to Samuel unto Ramah, and said unto him, behold, thou art old, and thy sons walk not in thy ways: now make us a King…And Samuel prayed unto the LORD. And the LORD said unto Samuel, hearken unto the voice of the people in all that they say unto you: for they have not rejected thee, but they have rejected me, that I should not reign over them."
>
> **[I Samuel 8:4-7]**

Beside the fact that God respects your will of choice, He is not limited to singling-out whoever He needs for His task. O yes! He proves His Godship over creation when there is a call

  CAPTURED BY HIS GLORY

for it. If you doubt this, ask Jonah.

A power-based life

Christianity is a power-based life [I Corinthians 4:20] built on faith [Hebrew 11:1-6], sustained by mercy [Lamentations 3:22-23]. It is not about the quantity of religious rites performed, but the quality of results produced. Results are effect of causes. It takes a life captured by His Glory to produce Kingdom results. Kingdom results are enduring results; they are results that defiles natural laws; results that bring you affluence and influence, and make you center of attraction, by the Holy Spirit! What kingdom results are you generating?

He would not do everything

God can do everything, but He would not. Being captured by His glory requires your deliberate participation. You have to create the atmosphere to be captured by His glory. This you do by:

1.   Making Yourself Available

While desire and determination serves as spring-board to achieving great feats; availability exposes you to the pitch where you face the reality of "players" you need to beat to score your goal. To be available is to be accessible. It is to be reachable, and be willing. God does not use the capable, but the available; if you are capable and available,

    CAPTURED BY HIS GLORY

you're on a solid vantage point.

> "And I sought for a man among them...But I found none..."
>
> **[Ezekiel 22:30]**

If there was one available, Sodom and Gomorrah would have not been destroyed. If there was one available to make up the hedge, and stood in the gap before the LORD, that sickness that had claimed almost everyone in your family would have been dealt with. If there was one available, your community would have been free from oppression. If there was one political leader [not ruler] available, a continent like Africa, so blessed with mineral and human resources would not be grappling with poverty and self-limiting acts. If there was a man... all God need is a man. He is a Spirit. He does not possess a physical body. He need your body, not everybody. You alone with God will make the difference desperately needed by the world. Are you available?

For every kingdom decision effected on earth, God used man; this has nothing to do with profession, position, location, qualification, language, colour, height, size or age. He qualifies the available and establishes their goings [Psalms 40:2], making them fit for His use.

     CAPTURED BY HIS GLORY

Making yourself available for God is making you accessible by Him. It is willingness to comply with His terms. You cannot serve God in your own terms. This is common with lots of believers today; they want to serve God in their own terms. It is no longer wrong cohabiting before marriage; some Church funds are mismanaged and used for personal gratification, it does not matter anymore. Christian mothers would abort their daughter's pregnancy gotten out of wedlock in order to cover shame, it doesn't matter anymore. You want to be noticed, "If it is not me, it is no one else." It has gotten to the point where some ministers send their wives packing while they camp "a daughter" who assumes the role of their wives. "I can marry and divorce when I want; it has nothing to do with my Christian faith," Really? A lot of Church people no longer live the prescriptions of scriptures, they are living their own terms. You cannot manipulate the Word of God; it is old, yet most recent. Get it right: you cannot serve God in your own terms!

Making yourself available is the point of giving everything about you for everything about God. It is the beginning of brokenness [Psalms 51:17] before God; a start of attracting the fullness of His glory; He never turns His eyes away from those available for Him.

          CAPTURED BY HIS GLORY

2.   Seeking His Face

It takes those who are available to seek the face of God. To seek simply means to look for. The Greek word is Zeteo. It means (to find out) by thinking, meditating, reasoning, to enquire into, seek after, seek for, aim at, strive after, require, demand, etc.

To be captured by His glory is to live His beauty and act His abilities. This would not be until you subject your being to seeking His face. To seek His Face is to lose your face. You cannot seek His Face and keep your face.

God has a hiding nature. Only those who seek Him find Him. It is written: "I love them that love me; and those that seek me early shall find me." [Proverbs 8:17]. Seeking Him entails:

a: Studying the Bible

The Bible is the Book that shelters the written word of God. It is old, yet current, and the only book that cannot be improved upon. It is the map to seeking God [Psalms 119:105]. A song writer calls it "a wonderful treasure; the gift of God without measure." You cannot find God outside His word. His word is the very essence of our salvation [John 1]. It carries in itself the ability to fulfill. Studying the bible builds hope and establishes in you, confidence to act faith. "This book of the law shall not depart out of thy mouth; but thou shalt meditate therein day and night, that thou mayest observe to do according to all that is written therein: for then thou shalt make thy way prosperous, and then thou shalt have good success." [Joshua 1:8].

b: Praying

This is a "Kingdom culture" all who seek to enjoy the awesomeness of God must live, and without ceasing [I Thessalonians 5:17]. Praying in this context means communicating, relating or fellowshipping with God. What you do is what you've learnt to do. If you don't know how to pray, you learn; like the disciples of Jesus Christ who requested that He teaches them how to pray [Luke 11:1]. You gain mastery when you are opened to learning.

There would be no fellowship or relationship without communication. Except it is a spiritual problem [even if it is], show me a failing marriage, I will show you a marriage with a failing communication. God is relationship oriented. He never created what He would not relate with. When you pray, you relate with God; relating with Him deepens your knowledge about Him and attract His "more" to your "less" [Exodus 33]. In praying, you should:

Pray in Songs

Songs of worship; not any kind of song; songs that appeal to

     CAPTURED BY HIS GLORY

your spirit and are directed to God alone; songs that lifts your spirit and create in you the sense of "it is not about me, but you, LORD;" Songs that brings you to complete brokenness. Many Christian song leaders don't know the power of a song; they sing latest songs [some of which the congregation don't know] and base their songs only on rhythm, which ends them entertaining without ministering. Although there is nothing wrong with entertaining, it makes you excited without delivering inner satisfaction. It is superficial. Mathematically, Lyrics plus Rhythm minus Desire equal Entertainment. Lyrics + Rhythm + Desire = ministration. The power of a song is your desire behind it, blended with motive.

Your motive is what sends your message, and God looks like the motive of your song. If the songs you chose to worship appeals to you, it appeals to God. You can fake praise, but you cannot fake worship. It is a heart-expression that consumes your total being. It consummates your relationship with God by the Holy Spirit. I call it "skin-to-skin" with the Father. God grants your needs when you pray literally, but gives you Himself when you worship. He said to Abraham, "…I am thy shield, and thy exceeding great reward." [Genesis 15:1]. You can imagine God being your reward, not gold [Haggai 2:8]. A lot of Church people don't know the importance of praying in songs, so they take it

     CAPTURED BY HIS GLORY

casual when praise and worship is on; but when literal prayer is engaged that God should kill their enemies, the ones that stood like "six O' clock" during praise and worship would start deceiving themselves.

Pray in Tongues

What an exceptional language that emboldens the believer? I make melodies and speak in tongues [I Corinthians 14:15] at the slightest prompt in my spirit, most especially when the picture is not clear to me. The outcome? Amazing results! Contrary to religious claims; there is absolutely nothing wrong with singing and praying in tongues [I Corinthians 14:18]. It is the language of angels [I Corinthians 13:1a] any born again believer, baptized in the Holy Spirit [Acts 2:3-4] is empowered [Romans 8:26] to speak, for sweet fellowship [II Corinthians 13:14c] with the Holy Spirit.

Tongues are spiritual IM [Instant Messages] encoded by you with the strongest encryption only the Holy Spirit can decrypt, decode and instantly act on. Don't let any religious dogmatic stand dissuade you from engaging the language of the Spirit. Speak-baby-speak, it edifies you! [I Corinthians 14:4a].

Pray with understanding

"I will pray with the spirit, and I will pray with the understanding also..." [I Corinthians 14:15]. Praying with

     CAPTURED BY HIS GLORY

understanding has nothing to do with multitude of words or vocabularies you know. Everybody can pray with understanding, but everybody may not have answered prayers.

The effectiveness of praying with understanding is a function of right application of the word of God during the act. You cannot pray amiss when guided by the word. God is committed to His word. "Rather than God's word fails, He will stop being God" (Anonymous): "…for thou hast magnified thy word above all thy name," (Psalms 138:2c). You commit God when you pray His word back to Him. Make praying your culture.

3.   Partner With The Holy Spirit

Activity without the Holy Spirit is religion. Religion is man- made; it breeds self-righteousness and conflict. There is no better partnership than that with the Holy Spirit. In Luke 24:49, Jesus Christ instructed the disciples to tarry in the City of Jerusalem, until they are endued with power from on high; and we read in Acts 1:12-14 & 2:1-43:

> "Then returned they unto Jerusalem from the Mount called Olivet, which is from Jerusalem a Sabbath day's journey...These all continued in one accord in prayer and supplication...suddenly there came a sound from heaven as of a rushing Mighty wind, and it filled all the house...and they were all filled with the Holy Ghost, and began to speak with other Tongues, as the spirit gave them utterance...But Peter, Standing up with the eleven, lifted up his voice..."

Peter, who denied Jesus trice as a result of fear in the scripture above, boldly declared Jesus as LORD and savior to the onlookers and over three thousand souls were saved by the words from his mouth. What will strengthen you to studying the word of God; praying with songs, tongues and understanding; manifesting God's glory powerfully than a veil could prevent [Exodus 34:30-35], and delivering kingdom dividends to the world, is your yieldedness to the Holy Spirit. The deeper your yieldedness, the higher you soar and show forth His praise.

Your nature will prevent you from partnering the Holy Spirit. When you yield yourself to Him, His nature increases [in you], and your nature decreases. The nature of Peter denied Jesus; but the nature of the Holy Spirit in Him publicly confessed Jesus as LORD, and thousands were saved. His nature made him drew out sword and smote the ear of a servant of the high priest; the nature of the Holy Spirit made him repairer of feeble body parts. His nature took him back to fisher of fishes; the nature of the Holy Spirit made him fishers of men. The more of the Holy Spirit you have, the brighter your life and ministry becomes.

4.   Study The Lives of God's Generals

Visit good Christian bookshops within your reach and buy books, tapes or CDs of those that shook their world for God's Kingdom. Do not be carried away by their glories. There is the story about their glory you need to know; that you would not find on the Pulpit, it is lying right in their books and tapes. Shelve their glory and study their stories, you would be amazed the stir it would cause in your spirit.

5.   Attend Inspiring Conferences

Attending conferences exposes you to opportunities that carry in them potentials to cause positive shift in your life. You get stirred by higher life messages and experience [first hand] the moving of the Holy Spirit by ministers captured by His Glory. You cannot stay in a Holy Spirit electrified atmosphere and not get electrified! You eventually become a conduit of His manifest power.

     CAPTURED BY HIS GLORY

6.   Serve In Your Church

Service is a virtue nothing can replace. To be captured by His Glory is to serve. This makes you responsible. Until you are ready to be responsible, you are not ready to be captured by His Glory. Responsibility is not undue burden, it is empowerment. Kingdom responsibility will not demand from you what was never created within you, however, it conditions you to handle truth which is really not just a thing one tells, but the purity of a beginning.

You cannot be captured by His Glory warming pew in the church. You must be functioning. You do not need to be a leader or an executive member of a department before you function. Service is what will take you there. If you are not serving, you are starving. You have not gotten the right dose of God's Word [Exodus 23:25-27] to stir you into service.

7.   Release The Anointing In You

You are a miracle packaged to happen to lives; these lives are eagerly waiting your manifestation. I once visited a couple for fellowship; against my wish the sister prepared a welcome meal. I eat the meal, blessed them and left for home. I revisited after a month and some weeks; this time I stood my ground I would not take anything except water. The sister subtly left the sitting room; I never knew she was going to make me meal. While she was out, the brother said, she told him that she must make me meal every time I visit. This was because; she discovered an unusual growth in her business after she prepared me a meal. Before they relocated, she ensured I visit every week. That is the anointing at work.

Two days after

We had counseled and prayed for them before the meeting. It was awesome as we worshipped. By the Holy Spirit, there was abundant word of knowledge and declarations. While I was soaked bottom-up as I perspire with little strength left in me [at the close of the meeting]; a woman I counseled and prayed for earlier insisted I pray for her husband [who was not present at the meeting].

"Madam, God has answered whatever prayer you want me to offer for your husband." I said. While she pressured, I asked her to leave that God will provide her husband a job within two months. She would not leave unless I touch her. I reluctantly held her hands and said: "go and watch God provide your husband a job within two months from tonight." "Amen!" she exclaimed and left. Two days after the declaration, her husband was called for an interview and asked to resume duty at the spot. This was according to her. She was happy and for her, I was a miracle sent her way. Many other testimonies emerged.

     CAPTURED BY HIS GLORY

Ulcerous

She had stomach ulcer for over two years. I was a Christian brother and regular client to the computing firm she worked. We talked and joked a lot whenever I visited until the day she narrated her ordeal. While I joked with her plight, she was very serious; I later became serious, too; held her hands, thanked God for her ordeal and commanded the stomach ulcer to heal; that was all. I heard her testimony elsewhere before she shared with me.

I was scared

There was a staff in her office with developing goiter, she called my attention to it telling me she believes God can use me heal her fiend. I was scared when I saw it; I down-played the effective power of the Holy Spirit at work in me by excusing myself of the scene. I could not remember it's not about me, but the Spirit of God at work in me.

Five or Six Singlet per day

He is a pilot, renown in his Church; the worship session was electrifying while the word of knowledge was released effortlessly, this was 2008. According to him, I spoke about someone who went for an appendectomy that was not properly done, and was dripping water-like substance, and I declared a supernatural correction of the same. He said, "I knew you were talking about my

      CAPTURED BY HIS GLORY

situation, but I took it with 'a pinch of salt.'" To his greatest surprise, he went to work the next day only to discover there was no need for a change of singlet. We ministered in that assembly August 2008, he called to share the testimony August 2009 [about a year after], and to be grateful for what God did for him through our visit. "You are a man of God," He said.

Not enough space to share more testimonies. These were all about the Holy Spirit, and me allowing Him reach men through me.

You need to understand that every challenge that comes your way is an opportunity to release the anointing in you. The anointing no longer reside in the Ark, it resides in you! It will not manifest until you release it. Reach out; release it and make profit for God's Kingdom. Your world awaits you!

5

WHEN CAPTURED
BY HIS GLORY

One major shift that occurs when you get captured by the glory of God, is that of purpose discovery. This is because God knows too well that purpose discovery is key to fulfillment in life. It is dangerous to be a part of nature's activities without knowing your course for life. The earth was founded on purpose. Purpose is the reason you are still alive. Until you discover your purpose for life, you're only existing and not living.

Moses, a frontier of the rescue mission of the children of Israel from their slave-drivers, spent about eighty years not knowing his course for life. When he noticed his murderous act was uncovered by an Israelite, he escaped for his life [Exodus 2:11- 15]. When you don't know your purpose you are prone to act right at wrong times on life issues. You run from place to place, business to business, church to church, relationship to relationship without being established.

As you continue in ignorance of the purpose you are born, you tend to think and act like life is trial by error. You settle for anything and end being nothing. You spend life instead of invest it! Little wonder we have "Nothing people" in this "Something world." You can't be captured by His glory and remain an existing being. His glory shifts

          CAPTURED BY HIS GLORY

you from existing to living being, as it opens you to purpose.

Moses found his course for life the day he was captured by the glory of God [Exodus 3:1-11], likewise, the Apostle Paul [Acts 9:1-20].

Purpose discovery is the start of relevance. Until you know and act purpose, you would be defectively relevant. Relevance is anchored on discovering and acting purpose; when you don't know the purpose you are born, you want to be 'everything' when you have not become 'one thing.' You fit-in the perfect description of a double minded being, as revealed in James 1:8

> "A double minded man is unstable in all his ways."

A double minded man is unstable not in one, two or three ways, but in all his ways. Relevance is far from such individual since focus is not acknowledged in his or her scheme of things.

Purpose selects. It determines the kind of life you live; the people with whom you flock; the places you go; the environment you live; career you choose and kind of person you marry.

Contrary to laid down principles of marriage by its

          CAPTURED BY HIS GLORY

originator [God], the rate at which couples are divorcing is recording geometric increase; the Church is not an exception!

A Pastor once told me that I am lucky for being single, as he shared his marital ordeal with me. According to him, he married at night, meaning, he made a wrong choice. He married a woman that is not of the same vision with him. Sometimes, it is 'war' persuading her to join him to Church. Sad enough, he was a Pastor before he met his wife that is now a 'knife' on his throat. What went wrong? Purpose was not factored in, at the time of choice. Those who shelve purpose for the physical content of a woman would certainly end up marrying at night; the reverse is also true.

Every marital union covenanted outside purpose would contend with more challenges than those covenanted on clean-clear-cut purpose. You are most likely to endure marriage when you marry someone that is not of the same vision or shared values. Until you have shared values, you are not meant for each other [Genesis 2:23]. You are likely to marry at night, make wrong friends, embark on wrong career choice, and build destructive relationships when you fail to discover your course for life.

You cannot be fulfilled outside the purpose you are born. I once asked a twenty seven year old acquaintance what her purpose is; her response was simple, "I don't know yet, and I have not started thinking about it."

My friend, God is interested in your life being fulfilled, and that fulfillment is in discovering and living the purpose you are born. No matter how old you are, you can start your purpose discovery process by allowing you captured by His glory. To be captured by God's glory is to know God. You need to know THE LORD [your maker] to know what you are created for. He knows more than anyone else, and every time you know Him, you know you.

6

DO THIS NOW!

The difference you need in your life, family, ministry, community, nation and the world is in being captured by His Glory. Wait a minute.

If you read through this book and know you are not born again. I am not saying you are not born again; you know it. I encourage you to make a decision to side with Jesus Christ right now. If you have decided; do this now:

> LORD Jesus. I call on You right now because I realize that life without You in its true sense worth nothing. I am a sinner and very sorry for not recognizing You in my life after all You did for me on Calvary. Forgive Me. Come be LORD and savior of my life, and fill me with the Holy Spirit as I start a new life with You. Thank You for saving me, in Jesus' Name! Amen!

If you just said the prayer above; I congratulate you. You are now born again. Not by religion, but by acceptance of Jesus Christ into your life. A child of God you are. A new creation: old things are passed away; behold, all things [about you] are become new (II Corinthians 5:17). Do not allow your past occupy the reality of your now; "there is therefore now no condemnation to them which are in Christ Jesus…" (Romans 8:1).

Your new faith will be challenged. Christianity is not a power struggle; it is a protest over truth. You need to be aware that protesting for truth is contending with forces of lies, but here is your assurance: "Ye are of God, little children, and have overcome them: because greater is He that is in you than he that is in the world!" (I John 4:4).

To be captured by His Glory is to serve and advance the Kingdom of God selflessly.

Thank You!

Sweet Holy Spirit

Mr. & Mrs. Amamy Efiri

Mr. & Mrs. Philip Odior

Rev. Alfred Odume

Pastor Evans Tobore

Rev. C. Kalu Ukpai

Ini Kingsley Ubong

Rev. & Mrs. Godfrey Okodugha